Thomas Jarrett

A New Way of Marking the Sounds of English Words without Change of Spelling

SALZWASSER
VERLAG

Thomas Jarrett

A New Way of Marking the Sounds of English Words without Change of Spelling

Reprint of the original, first published in 1859.

1st Edition 2022 | ISBN: 978-3-37513-158-6

Verlag (Publisher): Salzwasser Verlag GmbH, Zeilweg 44, 60439 Frankfurt, Deutschland
Vertretungsberechtigt (Authorized to represent): E. Roepke, Zeilweg 44, 60439 Frankfurt, Deutschland
Druck (Print): Books on Demand GmbH, In de Tarpen 42, 22848 Norderstedt, Deutschland

A NEW WAY OF MARKING

THE SOUNDS OF ENGLISH WORDS

WITHOUT CHANGE OF

SPELLING,

APPLIED IN

A SERIES Of PROGRESSIVE LESSONS.

A BOOK FOR CHILDREN, TEACHERS, AND FOREIGNERS.

BY THE

REV. THOMAS JARRETT, M. A.,

REGIUS PROFESSOR OF HEBREW IN THE UNIVERSITY OF CAMBRIDGE,
AND RECTOR OF TRUNCH, NORFOLK.

LONDON:

BERNARD QUARITCH,

CASTLE STREET, LEICESTER SQUARE.

—

1858.

THE following pages are designed to apply the Writer's "Method of marking the sounds of English words without changing the spelling." The system was devised by him more than eight years ago; and has been successfully used in a Village School for about half that time. The Writer believes that both Teachers and Learners will find their task much lessened by means of this method. The whole system being contained in the "Table of Similar Sounds," a person fully acquainted with this Table can read at sight any word marked according to this method. The Gospels and Acts have been printed so marked; and this little book is meant as an Introduction. The Teacher is requested to cause the Learner to go over each lesson till it has been thoroughly mastered. After the Learner has thus been accustomed to connect the spelling of English words with the proper sound of each word, the reading of books printed in the ordinary way becomes an easy task.

For the use of Foreigners who may wish to learn English, a Table has been printed, in which the English sounds are represented by words of the chief languages of Europe and Asia, as far as these sounds are contained in each language.

TRUNCH RECTORY,
Jan. 5, 1857.

ERRATA.

PAGE.	LINE.	ERROR.	CORRECTION.
1	5	bécáuse	bécáuśe
	10	that	thát
5	30	ıs	ıṡ
		final	final
8	6	no	not
12	7	gıve	ġıvẹ

A SHORT AND SURE WAY OF LEARNING TO READ.

1. In Ęnglısh thĕre arę twenty sıx letterś.

2. Fıve of theśe letterś arę called vowelś, that ıś, vȯcalś, or *voıce letterś*, becáuse they can be sounded alóne.

The vowelś arę,   A   E   Į   O   U.

                  a   e   ı   o   u.

Thĕır nameś arę, à   ė   i   ȯ   u̇.

3. Twenty ȯne letterś arę called consȯnants, that ıś, *wıth-sounderś*, becáuśe no ȯne of them can be sounded unléss ıt haś a vowel wıth ıt. The name of each of theśe consȯnants ıś made up of the letter ıtsélf, and a vowel eıther befóre or after ıt.

[1] Letterś whọśe sound ends theır name.		[2] Letterś whọśe sound begíns theır name.	
LETTER.	**NAME.**	**LETTER.**	**NAME.**
C c	ec	B b	bė
F f	ef	D d	dė
G g	eg	H h	hä
L l	el	J ȷ	jà
M m	em	K k	kà
N n	en	P p	pė
R r	är	Q q	cu̇
S s	es	T t	tė
X x	ex	V v	vė
		W w	waw
		Y y	yı
		Z z	zė or zed

4. Nearly every ȯne of the letterś haś more than ȯne sound. The dıfferent soundś of each letter arę shȯwn by dots and accents (´ \` ^).

5. Each vowel, when ıt haś ȯne dot ȯver ıt, ıś

* B

sounded like its name, and this sound is called its
name sound, as,

ė		i			ȯ		
bė	bind	hind	rind	ȯld	fȯld	bȯlt	rȯll
hė	blind	kind	grind	bȯld	hȯld	cȯlt	drȯll
mė	find	mind	wind	cȯld	tȯld	mȯst	strȯll

6. The vowels without any dot are sounded as in
the words nat, net, nit, not, nut. This sound is
called the *first sound* of each vowel.

a	e	ı	o	u	a	e	ı	o	u
am	em	ım	om	um	ap	ep	ıp	op	up
ham	hem	hım	hom	hum	hap	hep	hıp	hop	hup
yam	yem	yım	yom	yum	yap	yep	yıp	yop	yup
mam	mem	mım	mom	mum	map	mep	mıp	mop	mup
pam	pem	pım	pom	pum	pap	pep	pıp	pop	pup
bam	bem	bım	bom	bum	bap	bep	bıp	bop	bup
fam	fem	fım	fom	fum	fap	fep	fıp	fop	fup
vam	vem	vım	vom	vum	vap	vep	vıp	vop	vup
cam			com	cum	cap	kep	kıp	cop	cup
gam			gom	gum	gap			gop	gup
jam	jem	jım	jom	jum	jap	jep	jıp	jop	jup
lam	lem	lım	lom	lum	lap	lep	lıp	lop	lup
ram	rem	rım	rom	rum	rap	rep	rıp	rop	rup
sam	sem	sım	som	sum	sap	sep	sıp	sop	sup
tam	tem	tım	tom	tum	tap	tep	tıp	top	tup
	dem	dım	dom	dum	dap	dep	dıp	dop	dup
nam	nem	nım	nom	num	nap	nep	nıp	nop	nup
ab	eb	ıb	ob	ub	af	ev	ıf	ov	uf
hab	heb	hıb	hob	hub	haf	hev	hıf	hov	huf
yab	yeb	yıb	yob	yub	yaf	yev	yıf	yov	yuf
mab	meb	mıb	mob	mub	maf	mev	mıf	mov	muf
pab	peb	pıb	pob	pub	paf	pev	pıf	pov	puf
bab	beb	bıb	bob	bub	baf	bev	bıf	bov	buf
fab	feb	fıb	fob	fub	faf	fev	fıf	fov	fuf

a	e	ı	o	u	a	e	ı	o	u
vab	veb	vıb	vob	vub	vaf,	vev	vıf	vov	vuf
cab			cob	cub	caf			cov	cuf
gab			gob	gub	gaf			gov	guf
jab	jeb	jıb	job	jub	jaf	jev	jıf	jov	juf
lab	leb	lıb	lob	lub	laf	lev	lıf	lov	luf
rab	reb	rıb	rob	rub	raf	rev	rıf	rov	ruf
sab	seb	sıb	sob	sub	saf	sev	sıf	sov	suf
tab	teb	tıb	tob	tub	taf	tev	tıf	tov	tuf
dab	deb	dıb	dob	dub	daf	dev	dıf	dov	duf
nab	neb	nıb	nob	nub	naf	nev	nıf	nov	nuf
ac	ec	ıc	oc	uc	ag	eg	ıg	og	ug
hac	hec	hıc	hoc	huc	hag	heg	hıg	hog	hug
yac	yec	yıc	yoc	yuc	yag	yeg	yıg	yog	yug
mac	mec	mıc	moc	muc	mag	meg	mıg	mog	mug
pac	pec	pıc	poc	puc	pag	peg	pıg	pog	pug
bac	bec	bıc	boc	buc	bag	beg	bıg	bog	bug
fac	fec	fıc	foc		fag	feg	fıg	fog	fug
vac	vec	vıc	voc		vag	veg	vıg	vog	vug
	kec	kıc	coc	cuc	cag	keg	kıg	cog	cug
gac			goc	guc	gag			gog	gug
jac	jec	jıc	joc	juc	jag	jeg	jıg	jog	jug
lac	lec	lıc	loc	luc	lag	leg	lıg	log	lug
rac	rec	rıc	roc	ruc	rag	reg	rıg	rog	rug
sac	sec	sıc	soc	suc	sag	seg	sıg	sog	sug
tac	tec	tıc	toc	tuc	tag	teg	tıg	tog	tug
dac	dec	dıc	doc	duc	dag	deg	dıg	dog	dug
nac	nec	nıc	noc	nuc	nag	neg	nıg	nog	nug
al	el	ıl	ol	ul	as	es	ıs	os	us
hal	hel	hıl	hol	hul	has	hes	hıs	hos	hus
yal	yel	yıl	yol	yul	yas	yes	yıs	yos	yus
mal	mel	mıl	mol	mul	mas	mes	mıs	mos	mus
pal	pel	pıl	pol	pul	pas	pes		pos	pus
bal	bel	bıl	bol	bul	bas	bes	bıs	bos	bus

a	e	ı	o	u	a	e	ı	o	u
fal	fel	fıl	fol	ful	fas	fes	fıs	fos	fus
val	vel	vıl	vol	vul	vas	ves	vıs	vos	vus
cal			col	cul	cas			ços	cus
gal			gol	gul	gas			gos	gus
jal	jel	jıl	jol	jul	jas	jes	jıs	jos	jus
lal	lel	lıl	lol	lul	las	les	lıs	los	lus
ral	rel	rıl	rol	rul	ras	res	rıs	ros	rus
sal	sel	sıl	sol	sul	sas	ses	sıs	sos	sus
tal	tel	tıl	tol	tul	tas	tes	tıs	tos	tus
dal	del	dıl	dol	dul	das	des	dıs	dos	dus
nal	nel	nıl	nol	nul	nas	nes	nıs	nos	nus
at	et	ıt	ot	ut	ad	ed	ıd	od	ud
hat	het	hıt	hot	hut	had	hed	hıd	hod	hud
yat	yet	yıt	yot	yut	yad	yed	yıd	yod	yud
	wet	wıt	wot	wut		wed	wıd	wod	wud
mat	met	mıt	mot	mut	mad	med	mıd	mod	mud
pat	pet	pıt	pot	put	pad	ped	pıd	pod	pud
bat	bet	bıt	bot	but	bad	bed	bıd	bod	bud
fat	fet	fıt	fot	fut	fad	fed	fıd	fod	fud
vat	vet	vıt	vot	vut	vad	ved	vıd	vod	vud
cat	ket	kıt	cot	cut	cad	ked	kıd	cod	cud
gat			got	gut	gad				gud
jat	jet	jıt	jot	jut	jad	jed	jıd	jod	jud
lat	let	lıt	lot	lut	lad	led	lıd	lod	lud
rat	ret	rıt	rot	rut	rad	red	rıd	rod	rud
sat	set	sıt	sot	sut	sad	sed	sıd	sod	sud
tat	tet	tıt	tot	tut	tad	ted	tıd	tod	tud
dat	det	dıt	dot	dut	dad	ded	dıd	dod	dud
nat	net	nıt	not	nut	nad	ned	nıd	nod	nud
an	en	ın	on	un	man	men	mın	mon	mun
han	hen	hın	hon	hun	pan	pen	pın	pon	pun
yan	yen	yın	yon	yun	ban	ben	bın	bon	bun
	wen	wın	won	wun	fan	fen	fın	fon	fun

a	e	ı	o	u	a	e	ı	o	u
van	ven	vın	von	vun	ran	ren	rın	ron	run
can	ken	kın	con		san	sen	sın	son	sun
gan			gon	gun	tan	ten	tın	ton	tun
jan	jen	jın	jon	jun	dan	den	dın	don	dun
lan	len	lın	lon	lun	nan	nen	nın	non	nun

am	romp	drıp	trıck	gasp	rest	hunt
ram	mump	op	sıck	rasp	crest	and
cram	pump	rop	lock	grasp	test	hand
dram	jump	prop	clock	ask	mıst	band
amp	rump	crop	rock	mask	lıst	land
camp	crump	strop	frock	bask	cost	sand
lamp	ap	drop	crock	lask	rost	end
clamp	rap	ab	melt	flask	frost	wend
ramp	trap	rab	pelt	hast	must	mend
cramp	strap	crab	belt	mast	rust	bend
damp	ep	drab	felt	past	crust	lend
emp	tep	ack	held	vast	dust	rend
hemp	step	rack	urn	last	ant	send
ım	ıp	crack	burn	yest	ent	tend
rım	rıp	ıck	spurn	west	went	yond
brım	grıp	kıck	turn	pest	sent	pond
ımp	trıp	rıck	asp	best	tent	bond
lımp	strıp	brıck	hasp	vest	punt	fond

7. Änÿ letter wıth a sıngle dot under ıt ıs not sounded. A letter that ıs not sounded ıs saıd to be *silent;* as, b ın deḅt, lamḅ, comḅ, dumḅ.

8. An e wıthout änÿ mark ıs uṡually not sounded at the end of a wörd; as, twelve.

Thıs e ıs called a *silent e final.*

9. But an e not marked has ıts name sound at the end of a wörd of öne syllable, ın whıch thëre ıs no öther vowel; as,

be, he, me, we, ye.

LESSON I.

he can run. he led us. we fled from him. it will burn us. lift it up. we must send him. he can tell me. we must not run fast. he ran from ten men. he hid it from me. he trod on it, and it bit him. we did not tell him. he did not rob us. we must let him run. we must ask him. he did not run from us. a lamb ran from an óld man. a kid fled from a blind man. we must not bend it. he will tell me. we will not sell it. he tóld me. we will hóld him. he will bind it, and kill it. we must fóld it up. if we can find him, we will tell him. he will fill it. when will it be? he lost a cómb. we met a dumb man. he must mend a pén. we had a clock. he will send a lamp. he cut a rod. we must not romp. can he mend a crock?

10. An unmarked a, i, o, or u has its name sound if it is next befóre a silent e final, or if it is next befóre a single consónant which is follówed by a silent e final; as,

o in foe	a in babe	e in here	i in wide
woe	fade	mere	bite
u in due	made	mete	fire
	lake		hide
	make		life
	take		kite
	name		spite
	fame		bide
	lame		dine
	flame		fine
	same		file
	hate		mile
	base		side

o in robe	home	u in cure
bone	tone	pure
hope	stone	use
yoke	cone	tube
broke	cope	tune
rode	hole	mule
note	fore	mute

LESSON II.

a mad man made me run. it will fade. we must not take it. we gave him a name. fire will burn. he broke a bone. a mad man made a fire, and it burnt a babe in bed. we made him send it. a lad swam in a lake. he can cure us. we must hope. it will bite. we must hide it from him. we did not find life in it. it can hop, and we hope it will run. we must not climb on it. he fled from a foe. a dog will hide a bone. he stole a fat hen. he came home. we broke a lamp. he will take cold. a lame man ran a mile.

11. But the unmarked vowel keeps its first sound if the final e has a dot under it; as,

have, live, gone.

LESSON III.

he must have a run. we have land, and must till it. it must have milk. we can live here. he will have time.

12. An unmarked final o has its name sound; as, lo, no, so, go.

13. The pronoun I is sounded i.

14. The letter s, when it has ône dot över it, as s, is sounded like z, and may be called es, that is, ez; as, as, has, is, his, rise, wise.

8

no man can tell me. he tóld me so. go and find it. he is not in bed. he has left his home. he will have no more. did he not tell us so? he is not wise. he has no time. he came home at ten o'clock. we must no go till nine. he rose at five. he had no more. he left his babe in bed. we must ask him his name. he has not sent it, and so I have not got it. no wise man will act so. I can find no use in it. we must use it. I set my hat on a peg. we must hate no man. it is hot. I have not met him. he is gone.

15. *Accent.*—Thëre are three marks that are sömetimes set óver vowels:

        ✎ is called the acúte accent,
        ` is called the grave accent, and
        ^ is called the circumflex accent.

The acúte accent is set óver the first vowel of thát syllable, on which the stress of the voice must be laid in sounding a wörd. The grave accent döes not shów whëre the stress of the voice is to be laid, but ónly teaches how the vowel is to be sounded. The circumflex accent is made up of bóth the öthers, and shóws that the stress of the voice must be laid on the syllable whëre it is placed, and also that the vowel must be sounded as if a grave accent were on thát vowel. Thus, the stress of the voice must be laid on the secönd syllable in the follówing wörds:

atténd	défénd
abáse	dépénd
bëfóre	dèsîgn
conféss	dèsíre
dèclâre	offénd
défíle	próféss

All the letters and combinations of letters that have the s
are sounded alike.

1	a in hat		ee in feed	17	ȯ in wŏlf	28	m	
2	ä in father	eı	ceıl		ȯo good	29	c	
	äu äunt	ï	marine		ȯu cȯuld		ċ	
	ĕ clĕrk	ıe	field		ü püt		k	
	a arm	e	me	18	ėw in drėw		q	
3	ėy in ėye		mete		ọ dọ		ch	
	i bind		metes		oo moon	30	g	
	ẏ tÿrant		meted		ȯu yȯu		ġ	
	ı bıte	9	è in pȧper		ù trùth	31	ç	
	bıtes	10	ŏ in dŏne	19	y in yet		ch	
	y my		u but		ȩ dùteous		tch	
	ẏ dený	11	o in not		ı sȯldıer		t	
4	ȧ in ȧny		å wȧs		j hallelùjah	32	g	
	aı saıd	12	ò in form	20	ėau in bėauty		dg	
	ȧy sȧys	13	ạ in water		eu feud		J	
	e men		au fraud		ew new	33	l	
	ŭ bŭry		aw jaw		ù dùty	34	r	
5	ȧ in pȧper		ou brought		yȯu	35	s	
	ë whëre		a all		u dıspúte		c	
	ėı thėır	14	oı in voıd		dıspútes	36	ç	
	a hate		oy joy		dıspúted		cı	
	hates	15	eau in beau	21	w in wet		ch	
	hated		ėw sėw		ụ persuȧde		ş	
6	aı in paın		ȯ ȯld		u quıt		sh	
	ay day		oa boat	22	ŏ in ŏne, which is sounded wun		tı	
	ėa gréat		ȯw grȯw				t	
	ëı rëıns		o so	23	h in hat			
	ey they		oe toe	24	p in pen	37	ś	
7	ı in bıt		ough though	25	b in bıt		x	
	ȩ English		o note	26	f in fıne		z	
	ọ women		notes		ġh rouġh	38	m	
	ụ busy		noted		ph Phılıp			
	y hymn	16	ou in thou	27	f in of	39	nı	
	y happy		ow now		ph nejhew		ks	
é in évil			ough bough		v vex	40	x	
ea bead							gȥ	

nber in the following Table

			41	t in ten
1				d dreamed
ic			42	d n did
			43	th in thin
n			44	th in them
)l			45	th in eighth
			46	n in none
ônë			47	ng in long
			48	ng in lounge
l			49	ng in longer
ral			50	le in table
)			51	re in centre
			52	sion in mansion
				tion nation
				shun
			53	sion in invasion
				sun
			54	Silent letters :
n				[1] every letter
ious				having ône dot
iine				under it.
				[2] gh, having no
				mark.
al				[3] e, not marked
,				at the end of a
				word, unléss
ophon				thëre is no öther
				vowel in the
iure				same syllable.
e				[4] e, in the ter-
				mination es, un-
s				léss précéded by
t				cé, s, ch, sh, or
				y

a	1	è	9	k	29	r	34			
	2	ẹ	19	l	33	ṛ	51			
	5	ç	7	ḷ	50	s	35			
à	5	ea	8	m	28	ṡ	37			
ä	2	ėa	6	n	46	s̈	38			
ä	4	eau	15	ng	47	ṣ	36			
å	11	ėau	20	ṅg	48	sh	36			
ạ	13	ee	8	ng̈	49	t	41			
ạ̈	7	ei	8	o	11	ẗ	36			
ai	6	èi	5		12	ṭ	31			
ài	4	ëi	6		15	tch	31			
au	13	eu	20	ò	15	th	44			
äu	2	ew	20	ö	10	ṫh	43			
aw	13	ėw	15	ȯ	17	ti	36			
ay	6	èw	18	ö́	22	u	10			
ày	4	ey	6	ò	12		20			
b	25	ėy	3	ọ	18		21			
c	29	f	26	ọ	7	u̇	20			
	35	f	27	oa	15	ü	17			
ċ	29	g	30	oi	14	ü̇	4			
č	36		32	oo	18	ù	18			
ç	31	ġ	30	öo	17	ụ	21			
ch	31	gh	54	ou	16	v	27			
ċh	29	ġh	26	òu	18	w	21			
ëh	36	h	23	öu	17	x	39			
ci	36	i	3	ọu	13	ẋ	40			
d	42		7	ow	16	ẍ	37			
ḍ	41	i	3	ów	15	y	3			
dg	32	ï	8	oy	14		7			
e	4	ị	19	p	24		19			
	8	ie	8	ph	26	ẏ	3			
ė	8	j	32	ph	27	z	3			
ë	5	j	19	q	29	ż	38			
ẹ̈	2									

If thêre is no accent marked, the stress of the voice must be laid on the first syllable, unléss the word ends in ion. Thus, the stress of the voice must be laid on the first syllable of the following words :

camel	famine	visit
fragment	napkin	párents
hátred	timid	

The stress of the voice is söme-times called the accent.

16. The letter y becómes a vowel when thêre is no vowel in the same syllable, and also if it is at the end of a syllable. If it has no mark it is sounded like i, and if it has a dot óver it it is sounded like i ; as,

hymn	tyrant
dúty	
happy	

17. An unmarked final y is sounded like i, if it is at the end of a word of óne syllable, in which thêre is no öther vowel ; or if it is at the end of åny word, and has an accent óver it ; as,

by	try	applý	replý
fly	my	complý	relý
dry		dený	

18. If the letters wh begín a word, the h is sounded befóre the w; as, when, whip, white, why.

LESSON V.

he tóld me befóre. I cannot atténd. I will try. it is my dúty. we must not dený it. he is happy. if he will not let me, I cannot go. he must ask his párents when he can go home. tell me why he did not go. I came from my home at nine o'clock. I cannot fly, but I can run. I cannot write, but I will

try. a camel can travel in sand. I will replý. we
cannot relý on him. he will not complý. I depénd
on him, and he will defénd me. we must travel by
land. I cannot find my home. we cannot live here.
he will lamént. he must applý himsélf more. I
cannot atténd in time. it is a timid hare. I have
lost my knife.

19. When the letter c cömes befóre e, i, or y, it
is sounded like s, and is called cė, that is, sė; as,

face, city, price, cýpress.

When the letter g cömes befóre e, i, or y, it is
sounded like j, and is called gė, that is, jė; as,

age, rage, rigid, regent.

These sounds of cė and gė are called soft sounds;
and the sounds of ec and eg are called hard.

But if thëre is a dot óver the c or g, it keeps its
hard sound, and is called eg, éven when follówed by
e, i, or y; as, get, give, begín, forgét, forgíve.

20. The letters c and g keep thèir soft sound
befóre an e with a dot under it, and have thèir hard
sound befóre a, u, or h, with a dot under it; as,

guest   ghóst
guide
guile
guilt
plágue

LESSON VI.

I set my hat in its place. he struck me in my
face. we can slide on ice. he tóld me his age. he
is in a rage. he fell and cut his face. get up and
give me a pen. he is my guest. I will guide him.
he has no guile in him. I conféss I am guilty. we
must not plágue him. he is guiltless.

21. When the letter h follows c, g, p, s, or t, it loses its own sound, and the two letters together make a new sound, and they have a name belonging to the double letter. The double letter must, in spelling, be treated as one letter.

22. The double letter sh is called esh; as,

fish	she	shame	dish	shin	shop
brush	ship	shut	wish	shine	shape

23. The three letters tch make but one sound, which is called etch; as,

batch, catch, latch, latchet, fetch, ditch, stitch, witch.

24. The double letter ch has three sounds, and a name for each sound ; as,

[1] without any mark, it is called chè, that is, tchè :

chime	lurch
chin	much
chip	such
child	rich
chose	which
church	

[2] with a dot over the c it is sounded like k, and is called chè, that is, kè; as,

ache, echo, scheme.

[3] with two dots over the c it is sounded like sh, and is called chè, that is, shè ; as,

bench	branch
bunch	flinch
	trench

25. The double letter th has two sounds and two names :

[1] without a mark it is called thè ; as,

them, then, than, this, that, these, those.

[2] wıth a dot óver the t ıts name ıṡ eth ; aṡ,
bóth, cloth, thın, thıck.

Becáuṡe the wörd "that" haṡ several meanıngṡ, an
accent ıṡ püt óver ıt when ıt ıṡ the oppoṡıtę oḟ "thıs."

LESSON VII.

she must go home. she wıll not find ıt. when
dıd she gıve hım the pen ? shut ıt up. ıt ıṡ a shame.
brush my hat. thıs child came wıth me. he choṡe
thát pen. why dıd he tell us thát sad stóry ? he ıṡ
such a bad child, that he must go home. thıs ıṡ the
man that we met. whıch ıṡ the man that tóld us
thát tale ? I am not rıch. the shıp wıll go on the
lake. we must shut the bag. I cannot catch fish.
ıt ıṡ ın the dıtch. make fast the latch. we came
back from church. my face wıll áċhe. he can sıt
on a benċh. gıvę hım a bunċh. take thıs branċh.
cut a wıde trenċh. gıvę them the pen. take up the
pın. wıpe up thát blot. thát cloth ıṡ thın. thıs
plate ıṡ thıck. bóth can go. we must not flınċh.
thát ıṡ not a bad sċheme. the bellṡ wıll chıme. he
cut hıṡ thumḅ. she must take the cloth. I shun
such a bad child. he fed hıṡ child on rıce. he left
us ın the lurch.

26. The doubḷe letter ph ıṡ sounded lıke f, and ıṡ
named phi, that ıṡ, fi ; aṡ,
Phılıp, phılósopher.

27. An f wıth a dot óver ıt ıṡ sounded lıke v ; aṡ, oḟ.

28. The doubḷe letter gh, when ıt haṡ no mark óver
ıt, ıṡ not sounded, and ıṡ called eg, hä ; aṡ, dough,
whıch ıṡ sounded dȯ, and though, sounded thȯ.

The doubḷe letter gh, when ıt haṡ a dot óver ıt, ıṡ
sounded lıke f, and ıṡ called ġhė, that ıṡ, fė ; aṡ, rọuġh,
whıch ıṡ sounded ruf.

29. The double letter dg is sounded like j, and is called edge, that is, ej ; as,

hedge	judge	sedge
grudge	pledge	wedge

LESSON VIII.

both of them might sit on the same bench. Philip is a wise philósopher. it is a bright night. we might find him. the light is gone. it is a sad sight. I have lost the lash of my whip. it is of an odd shape. she is shy. I live more in the sun than in the shade. she must fetch rice from the shop. he shot a timid hare. the sun will shine brightly. he set the hot fish on a cold dish. he came wet from the ditch. we will chat with him. he cannot tell us the depth of the pit. he struck it thrice. she will clothe him in black. make this rope tight. that is not right. fetch a match, and get a light. stretch this cloth. I cannot judge him. she will grudge us. I set it on its edge. she will dry that napkin on the hedge. he will send us a pledge. I will drive this wedge. she must light the fire with sedge.

30. The double letter ng is called eng ; as,

bring	sing	long	thing	throng
hang	song	strong	thong	wrong

31. If a dot is placed over the n in ng, each letter is sounded separately, and they are spelled en, ge; as, angel, change, range, strange, hinge, singe.

32. When an n comes before g, k, q, or x, it is sounded as ng (eng); as, longest, strongest, bank, rank, think, drink, sink. But the n keeps its proper sound when it has a dot over it; as, mankind.

LESSON IX.

he sits on a bank. she will thank him. we must

not thınk hım so bad. the shıp wıll sınk ın the lake. she wıll not drınk thát mılk. he ıs strong. my tıme ıs not long. ıt ıs a stráṅge thıng. he must cháṅge hıs place. she tóld me a long tale. he wıll sıng a song. thát plank ıs thıck. thát rope ıs the stroṅgest of the ẉhole. thıs ıs the loṅgest lıne. she ıs aṅġry at us.

33. The vowels wıth twọ dots óver them arẹ sounded aṡ follóẇs :

ä	ë	ï	ö	ü
bälm	ëre	maríne	abóve	büll
hälf	thëre	machíne	cöme	büsh
pälm	whëre	ravíne	döne	büshel
psälm			döve	füll
			löve	püll
				püt

34. The vowels wıth twọ dots under them arẹ sounded aṡ follóẇs :

a̤	e̤	ḷ	ọ	ṳ
ta̤lk	dúteọus	chrıstạan	dọ	dıssṳáde
wa̤lk			lọṡe	
wa̤r			mọve	
wa̤rm			prọve	
wa̤rn			shọe	
ẉra̤th			ẉhọ	

ġıvẹ me hälf of ıt. I havẹ cut the pälm of my hand. he sang a long psälm. I am not wạrm. we must wạrn hım. wạr ıs a sad thıng. he must not ta̤lk. cöme and take a wa̤lk wıth me. we met hım thëre. whëre can I find ıt? I havẹ not döne so. we wıll not dọ ıt. ẉhọ wıll cöme wıth me? take off my shọe. he ran tọ and fro. here ıs a döve. dọ not lọṡe my glöve. she dıd not löve hım. ıt ıs abóve me. she strove tọ take ıt from me. I thınk ıt ıs

not well tọ dọ so. we wıll gívẹ ıt tọ hım. wıll she
cöme wıth me ? we wıll prọve ıt tọ hım. I cannot
mọve ıt. püt ıt on the desk. püll off my shọe. my
hand ıṡ füll. thát ıṡ a wild büll. I met söme oȉ
them thëre. he wıll not cöme alóne. dọ not lọṡe
the place. he haṡ lost the ónly thıng we gave hım.
we must wạrn hım not tọ dọ so. cut off a branëh
from thát büsh. dọ not püsh so. püt the rıce ın a
büshel. she wıll dıssụáde hım from such conduct.
he ıṡ füll oȉ wrạth. she ıṡ wróth at thát. I cannot
grasp thát wıth my mind. he haṡ bróken the hıṅge.
she ıṡ sıngıng whıle she sıts by the fıre, and ıṡ sıṅgẹ-
ıng the dreṡ .

35. The letter u wıth a grave accent ıṡ sounded
lıke ọ ; aṡ,

trùth, trùly, trùe.

36. The vowelṡ wıth three dots óver them arẹ
sounded aṡ follówṡ :

ä̇ lıke e ; aṡ, ä̇ny, mä̇ny.

ė̈ lıke ä ; aṡ, clė̈rk.

ȯ̈ lıke ü ; aṡ, wȯ̈lf, wȯ̈man.

u̇̈ lıke e ; aṡ, bu̇̈ry.

37. The vowelṡ wıth three dots under them arẹ all
sounded lıke ı ; aṡ,

Ẹnglısh, bụṡy, wọmẹn.

38. The vowel å ıṡ sounded lıke o ; aṡ,

wånt, wåṡ, wåsh, wåtch, whåt.

39. The vowel ȯ ıṡ sounded lıke wu ; aṡ,

ȯne, ȯnce.

40. An unmarked a, follówed by ll, ıṡ sounded
lıke ạ ; aṡ,

all, call, fall, gall, hall, small, wall.

But the a keeps its *first sound* if thëre is a dot
under the secönd l; as, shall.

she must tell the whole trùth. I do not thınk that
ıt ıs trùe. he spoke trùly. she ıs not trùthfùl. he
wıll tell thát to all men. ıt wıll be of no use to call
hım yet. he must take care not to fall. she sat ın
the hall. we can walk home. he went back to find
the ball. shall I gıve hım the pen ? she shall not
go wıth me. he wıll not try to wörk. wıll he also
cöme ? I cannot find åny thıng thëre. she dıd not
püt mǎny pens ın the desk. mǎny men wıll cöme
back. have we lost åny thıng ? she ıs a tall wöman.
the dog ran from a wölf. we met five tall women.
she cannot talk Englısh. we shall be bu̇sy. who
wıll bu̇ry hım ? I thınk ıt wås a sad tale. he must
wåsh hıs hands. I have lost my wåtch. we do not
wånt to go home. we wısh to lıve here. Thëre ıs
the wöman that we came to talk wıth. I have not
met more than ône man ın all my walk. I have püt
ône pen ın my desk. she püt two caps ın thát place.
we püt three hats thëre. she met us ônly ônce.

41. The letter r often chånges the sound of the
vowel befóre ıt.

[1] The letters ar are sounded lıke är ın a wörd
of ône syllable, or ın åny syllable that has the
accent ; as,

are	large	barn	farmıng
far	mark	star	alármıng
guard	arm	part	
hard	farm		

But the a ın ar keeps its *first sound* if the next
letter ıs either an öther r or a vowel ; as,

carry, marry, tarry.

[2] The letters er and ir are sounded nearly like ur; as,

herb	were	birth	anger	fäther	mȧnger
herd	bird	first	longer	möther	messenger
her	gird	adder	answer	bröther	strȧnger
err	third	after	scatter	sister	stronger

But if the syllable er or ir is followed by a syllable beginning with an öther r, or with a vowel, and has the accent, the *first sound* of e or i is kept; as,

merry, very, irrégular.

[3] The letters or are sounded nearly like ar in a wörd of ône syllable, or in ȧny syllable that has the accent; as,

form	lord	forty
storm	thorn	morning
corn	sort	orphan
horn	north	

But the o in or keeps its *first sound* if the next syllable begins with an öther r, or with a vowel; as,

sorry, forest.

LESSON XII.

it is not far to go. it wȧs in the barn. thȧt star is very bright. he wörks on the farm. he broke his arm. we are not far from home. she will guard him from all harm. she gave him a large part of whȧt she had. we made a mark in the place. he left it in the barn. she must not carry it back to him. why did he tarry so long? he gave her a pen. she cut söme herbs. he has flocks and herds. we must not err from the right pȧth. we were glad he did not cöme. the bird wȧs in her nest. this is the third time. I came first, and he did not cöme

* D

tıll long after me. my fäther and möther arę lıvıng
here, but my bröther and sıster wıll lıvę thëre a much
lonġer tıme. dıd he call on the strånġer? thëre
wås not much dánġer. he püt ıt ın the mánġer.
she must arrânġe ıt wıth more care. she ıṡ very
merry, and we arę not very sorry. we must dǫ aṡ
we arę bıd. the wınd ıṡ from the north. we must
ġo förth. thëre wıll be a storm. he wıll grind söme
corn. he ıṡ wındıng söme twıne. thát büll haṡ lost
ône of hıṡ hornṡ. I havę hurt my fınġer wıth a
ihorn. he must dǫ nöthıng of the sort. we shall
find more than fơrty of them. whåt shall we fínd ın
the forest? I must not forġét my bag. I hope he
wıll forġívę me. I thınk thıs ıṡ the longest chåmber.
thıs letter ıṡ wrıtten on very thın påper. he wrote
the wıll on parchment. he haṡ not wrıtten a quạrter
aṡ much aṡ I havę.

42. When twǫ dots arę placed under an l or r, the
l or r ıṡ tǫ be sounded after the vowel that follòwṡ ıt,
and the e ın ļe or ŗe ıṡ sounded very short; aṡ,

áble	temple	centŗe	ıŗön
càble			
sımple			
tàble			

43. If a wörd endṡ ın eṡ, the e ıṡ sılent, unléss ıt
follòwṡ c (cė), s, ch, sh, or x; and the vowel next
befóre the e must be sounded aṡ ıf the ṡ werę not
thëre; aṡ,

döve	döveṡ	drıve	drıveṡ	bıte	bıtes
face	faceṡ	lıfe	lıveṡ		
roṡe	roṡeṡ	fısh	fısheṡ		

44. If a wörd endṡ ın ed, the e ıṡ generally not
sounded, unléss the letter befóre ıt ıṡ eıther d or t;

and the vowel next befóre the e must be sounded aś
if the d werę not thëre ; aś,
arríve, arríved ; prıze, prızed ; divért, divérted.

LESSON XIII.

she ıś not áblẹ tọ dọ thát. ıt wıll fall from the
táblẹ. whåt a sımplẹ child ıt ıś ! thıs ıś the centrẹ
óf the cırclẹ. the smıth haś made a shọe for the
horse. he made ıt from part óf a bar óf irọ̈n. I
wås unáblẹ tọ tell hım at whåt tıme he might cöme.
here arẹ twọ döveś. she löveś the lıttlẹ child very
much. she lıveś far from us. we hope tọ spend
better lıveś. the lıveś óf five men werẹ lost thëre.
thát man drıveś twọ horseś. she haś five rośeś.
hıś fäther haś wörked at mäny placeś. söme fisheś
lıvẹ ın sạlt wạter, and ötherś ın fresh. he lıvẹd ın
this place a very long tıme. råvenś arẹ very long-
lıved. she tạlked wıth me a lıttlẹ whıle. we wạlked
ın the garden wıth hıś möther. her fäther deśíred
me tọ brıng hım söme rośeś. she tạlks very glıbly,
but döeś not wörk well. her töngue ıś more actıvẹ
than her fiṅgerś.

45. The letter ţ ıs sounded lıke ch ;. aś,
naţural.

46. The letter ş ıś sounded lıke sh ; aś,
şùre, şùrẹly.

47. The letter ş̈ ıś sounded nearly lıke zy (y bëïng
a consónant); aś,
meạ̈surẹ, treạ̈surẹ.

48. The letter. q ıś ạlwayś sounded lıke k; and qu
arẹ sounded lıke kw ; aś,

quıt	réquíre	conquẹr
quıte	rẹquést	

* D 2

49. The letter x has three sounds :

[1.] When unmarked, like ks ; as,

    tax

    wax

    flax

    six

    vex

[2.] With ône dot óver it, like gz ; as,

    exáct   exâlt

    exámine   exúlt

[3.] With two dots óver it, like z ; as,

    Xenophon.

LESSON XIV.

it is not natural to do so. she is an unnátural
möther. whât is the náture of the plan ? who can
meáșure it ? it is a vast treáșure. I cannot find
âny pleáșure in such a wörk. I am șùre it is not
safe to wa̧lk here. șùrely she can tell me whère she
püt it. the child will not quit its möther. I rè-
quésted him to cöme. he döes not requíre thát of
me. here are six boxes. he had two foxes. I
went into the garden that I might gather söme flax,
but I gathered very little. I cannot find the wax.
we must not vex him. she is very exáct. he will
exámine whât I have written. he will be exâlted to
a lofty place. we will be glad, exúlt and sing. I am
not áble to fix it in its proper place. mix this wa̧ter
with the milk. he shall cöme next to her. whât
wâs the text? she met six oxen. the foxes stole
six hens. püt the yoke on the neck of the ox. the
águe is bad enoúgh, but the plágue is much wörse.
cleanse thát cloth.

50. The letters ion are sounded like yun;
the letters sion and tion are sounded like shun; and
the letters sion are sounded like sun.

The stress of the voice must always be placed on
the syllable next before ion.

If the i on ion has any mark, its sound will be
known by that mark.

union	mansion	nation	confusion	lion
dominion	passion	position	persuasion	question
		notion	evasion	
		motion		
		lotion		

The letters ti and ci when before an unmarked
a, i, o, or u are sounded like sh; as,

martial   gracious
partial

LESSON XV.

we must unite in completing the work, for union
is strength. here are some onions. he will have
dominion over all in the land. she must not do such
a bad action. he did not mention it to me. he has
an odd notion. where did I put the potion that was
sent for the child to drink? here is the lotion to
wash his bad leg with. he has come from the station.
she has lost her situation, and cannot get an other
place. what is his condition? she is in addition,
he is in subtraction, and I am in multiplication; but
division is much harder. we must not be in a
passion. what a strange confusion! others told me
so. it was not the same dog but an other. we had
no provisions with us. it was a national calamity.
she was very partial. he sang a martial song. the
man is very gracious.

51. When twọ vowels cöme tọgéther ın the same syllabḷe they arẹ called a dıphthong. The letter w söme-tımeś formś part of a dıphthong, havıng the efféct of u.

52. Söme-tımeś ône of the vowelś ıś marked aś sılent, and ıś thëre-forẹ not sounded ; aś,

aịr	faịr	teảr
bẹảr	frịend	trọubḷe
deạd	haịr	wẹảr
deạth	heạd	yẹả
dòọr	paịr	
dọubḷe	pòụr	

LESSON XVI.

my òld frịend ıś deạd. dọ not strıke my heạd. I cannot bẹảr ıt. we met a dancıng bẹảr. we shalḷ wẹảr black clòtheś. shut the dòọr. here ıś a paịr of shọeś. let us waḷk ın the fresh aịr. pòụr söme wạter on my handś. I wıll còmḅ my haịr a secönd tıme. he wıll gịvẹ me dọubḷe the làbọur that she dıd. dọ not trọubḷe hım so much.

53. ea, ee, eı, and ıe arẹ all sounded lıke ė ; aś,

ea	ee	eı	ıe
beat	deed	ceıl	bėlíef
each	feed	seıze	bėlíeve
east	flee	concéıve	chıef
feast	free	dėcéıve	field
heat	heed	percéıve	fierce
ḳnead	ḳnce	récéıve	grıef
leaf	need	concéıt	grıeve
meat	see	dėcéıt	shıeld
peace	thee	récéıpt	thıef
sea	three		wıeld
seat	tree		
tea			

LESSON XVII.

we walked by the sea. she came to see us. he
drank tea with us. here is a rose leaf. each of us
must go to his seat. we shall have a treat. the
heat makes me wish to sit in the shade. she has no
meat to eat. the sun rises in the east. we must
not quarrel, but be at peace with each öther. the
child sits on the knee of its möther. here are three
roses. she will flee from them. let us sit under
the tree. give heed to what he tells us. thëre is
no need to do thát. I cannot see whëre it is. cöme
and feed the baby. that was a strange deed. he
was felling a tree, and it fell on him, and it almòst
killed him. his feet are so weak that he is not able
to walk. he seized the robber, and püt him in
prison. I cannot wish to deceíve him, and so I will
tell him all the trùth. when will he receíve his
wages? he fears to face the foe. I see guilt in his
face. I do not belíeve it. let us go into the field.
this is the chief thing. it made him grieve much.
he was a thief, and stole what was in the bag. it
was a strong but small shield. this is so long a
weapön that he cannot wield it.

54. ëi is sounded like à; as,

            hëir, thëir.

55. ëy is sounded like i; as,

            ëye.

LESSON XVIII.

this little child is hëir to a large estáte. thëir
fäther and möther are both dead. he struck me
betwéen my ëyes. she cannot close her ëyes.

56. au, aw, and ọu arẹ sounded like ạ; aṡ,

aught	dawn	brọught
caught	draw	nọught
cauṡe	law	ọught
naughty	saw	sọught
slaughter		thọught

57. äu iṡ sounded like ä; aṡ,

äunt
dräuġht
läuġh
läuġhter

LESSON XIX.

whȧt wȧṡ the cauṡe of thát mistáke? I cannot tell him aught on the subject. we caught mȧny fisheṡ. thëre wȧṡ a frightfül slaughter. the law iṡ very clear on thát matter. we saw the whole battle, and a shockıng sight ıt wȧṡ. thát horse cannot draw the cart. the dawn bėgán tọ appéar. she ọught not tọ dọ such a thıng. we brọught hım home. I can see nọught tọ justıfẏ her conduct. she sọught her child wıth mȧny tearṡ. she must not tẹȧr her frock. wė thọught ıt might dọ sӧme harm. hıṡ äunt and hıṡ uncle werẹ wạlkıng ın the garden, and trampled on a number of ants. why dıd she läuġh so much? perháps ıt wȧṡ tọ try by her läuġhter tọ hıde a sad hẹart; but ıt ıṡ a hard thıng quıte tọ concéal the feelıngṡ. she gave hım a dräuġht of cȯld wạter. he drank sӧme wạrm tea. the doctӧr sent hım a dräuġht ın a bottle, tọ cure a cȯld he had caught by sıttıng ın a dräuġht of wınd when he wȧṡ wạrm. thıṡ wȧṡ thọughtless and unwíṡe.

58. èau, eu, and ew, are sounded like ů; aś,

beauty	feud	dew
bèautiful		few
		ḳnew
		new
		vıew

LESSON XX.

ıt ıś wrong to stır up feudś. we must try to end quårrelś quıckly. thëre ıś a heavy dew on the grass. she ḳnew hım not ın hıś new dress. few persönś have so fıne a vıew. whåt a bèauty! never have I heard such bèautifůl můsıc.

59. eau, èw, oa, and ȯw, are sounded like ȯ; aś,

beau	sèw	board	blȯw.
		boat	flȯw
		float	grȯw
		moat	ḳnȯw
		throat	ȯwe
			slȯw
			sȯw.

LESSON XXI.

he ıś such a beau ın hıś new dress. she must sèw her frock, and he wıll sȯw the seedś. the wınd bègán to blȯw. the waterś flȯw very slȯwly. the treeś have ceased grȯwıng. no man can ḳnȯw thát. we ȯwe hım a debt of thanḳfůlness. the waveś tossed the boat. he seızed me by the throat. thıs vessel can hardly float. thëre ıś but lıttle water ın the moat. thıs board haś been bored fůll of holeś. thëre ıś very lıttle snȯw ın thát field. he went abroåd, to escápe from those to whom he ȯwed möney.

* E

60. ŏo and öu arę sounded like ü; aś,

bŏok	cöuļd
föod	shöuļd
föot	wöuļd
göod	
löok	
stöod	
töok	
wöod	

LESSON XXII.

thát iś a very göod bŏok.   he stöod wıth ône föot ın the boat and the öther on the shore.   thıs flesh iś not göod for föod.   löok at thıs béautıfül bŏok. she shöuļd not taļk so fast.   why cöuļd he not sıt stıll ın hıś seat ?   cöuļd she cöme, ıf I werę tǫ ınvíte her ? I cannot see why yóu shöuļd be so anǵry for so trıflıng a fault.   the poor ġırl cöuļd hardly avóıd ıt. I ihınk that thát "thát" that thát gentļeman uśed ǫught tǫ havę been "whıch."

60. oo, óu. and èw, arę sounded like ù ; aś,

loose	ihróugh	drèw
moon	yóu	thrèw
noon	yóur	wıthdrêw
smooth	yóuih	
soon		
too		

LESSON XXIII.

dıd yóu tell me trùly, why ıt wâś yóu dıd not cöme ? yóur făther wıll be thëre.   hıś yóuih iś no excúse for such folly; though söme persönś perháps wıll be reądy tǫ excúśe hım.   ıt iś pleąśant tǫ waļk by the light of the moon.   the horse soon broke loose, and ran back to the stable. whåt a smooth sea! thróugh the whole afternóon the sun has been too hot for a cömförtable walk. he drèw me asíde, tóld his tale, and then withdrêw from the room. he thrèw a stone into the water. the swållóws will soon take their flight. I hope to-morrów will be a fine day. he hopes to be åble to shoot söme partridges amóng the turnips. thát bird hops alóng on the high road. his dog will fetch and carry almóst åny thing that is not too big or too heavy. I cöuld not complý with his desíre. yóu wöuld not conféss yóur fault, as yóu ought to have döne.

61. ai, ay, ėa, ëi, and ey, are sounded alíke; as,

fain	day	bréak	fëign	prey
faith	hay	gréat	rëign	they
hail	may		rëins	convéy
laid	pay		wëigh	survéy
maid	pray		ëight	
nail	say			
pain	bétráy			
rain				
sail				
tail				

62. åi and åy are sounded like the *first sound* of e; as,

agåin	sàys
agåinst	
såid	
såith	

LESSON XXIV.

I püt no faith in his fàir speeches. the hail fell for a short time; but, when the wind chànged, it wås succéeded by rain. he hung his coat on a nail in the

wall. when the wind wås high, and the sea rough,
he töok up the mast, and laid it, with the sail, in the
bottöm of the boat. the little maid wås caught in
the rain. the whole day has been ône of hail and
snów. may I say that yóu will cöme soon? thëre
will be a grèat storm; and I shöuld advíse yóu tọ
make hàste home. cut up this wöod, and brèak these
branöhes. gather söme kindling, tọ light a fire for
yóur breakfast. dọ not fëign tọ knòw whàt yóu are
ignórant of. I wöuld fain know why he did not
cöme. no king is likely tọ rëign a grèat màny years.
wëigh well yóur wörds befóre yóu speak. they are
like hungry wölves, greedy after prey. he must pay
whàt is due tọ yóu. they sàid that it wås impóssible
tọ reach the place in göod time. yóu must cöme
agåin soon. he ran agåinst me in the twilight. she
sàys yóu ọught not tọ go. she püt on her vëil. he
sàid she wås a widòw. he gave me a very ugly blòw.
the wöman seems almóst cràzy. he came tọ bid me
adịéu. the weather is very hàzy; we can hardly
distínguish åny thing a few yards off. gịve him
söme-thing tọ assụáge his pain. yóu must be on yóur
guard agåinst such faults.

63. oi and oy are sounded alíke; as,

boil	boy
broil	joy
join	toy
noise	annóy
voice	dèstróy
void	
avóid	

LESSON XXV.

speak with a gentle voice; and dọ not make so grèat

a noiśe. boil the beef, and broil the fish. yòu seem tọ be void of understándıng. dọ yòu not ķnòw that yòu ọught tọ behàve more wiṣẹly? a naughty boy wıll speedıly dọ mıschıef. thıs wıll püt an end tọ all our joy. a child ıṡ not long pleaṡed wıth the same toy; ıt brèaks ône, and then wånts an öther. we must avóıd ġıvıng troubḷe. I saw a boy that wåṡ deạf and dumḅ. the haıl may dèstróy the ẹhole crop. dọ not annóy hım ın thát way.

64. ou and ow arẹ sounded alíke; aṡ,

bough	house	bow	how
cloud	houṡeṡ	brow	now
drought	loud	drown	vow
found	plough	fowl	
	thou		

LESSON XXVI.

he wıll bow down. he haṡ bent hıṡ bòw, and made ıt reạdy. now we wıll löok for the lonġest bough on thıs tree. we shalḷ soon see how tọ dọ ıt. she sat down ın the mıddḷe of the room. he found the sow amóng the flower-bedṡ. whåt fıne fowlṡ theṡe arẹ! how mǎny houṡeṡ arẹ thëre here! whåt a dark cloud ıṡ behînd the town! how loud the ẹhunder sounded! befóre we sòw the land, we must plough ıt well. be càrẹfül tọ make straıght furròwṡ. the seed that he sòwed dıd not gròw, on accóunt of the grèat drought. the high wınd caught the saıl, and upsét the lıttḷe boat; so that the twọ boyṡ, ẹhọ cöuḷd not swım, werẹ drowned. thıs cauṡed grèat sorròw tọ the pàrents of bòth the poor fellòwṡ. they werẹ bürıẹd, at the same tıme, ın a church-yard that lıeṡ on the brow of the hıll òver-löokıng the sea. he ıṡ a lázy man, and will neither plough nor sòw. almòst all men gain their bread either by the sweat of their brow, or the toil of their brain ; and they who are not oblíged to wörk for their föod, must find söme emplóyment for themsélves, in order to présérve their health. thëre is a grèat quántity of snòw on the ground. löok on thát cròw, which is perched on the highest bough of the tree. the cock bégán to cròw. the flowers will soon òpen, if we ġet a few warm showers. they wåndered from house to house, and from chåmber to chåmber. thát road is dångerous on accóunt of the nearness of the cliffs. light me a candle from thát wax táper. be cáreful not to squåbble abóut trifles. he squåndered his mönęy, by spending it on things he did not wånt. wáste not, wånt not. he tied the mule to the månger, by a halter that wås too weak to hòld the animal ; and so it quickly broke loose, and ran to the pond, to ġet a dräught of water. poor thing! it wås very thirsty. I cannot quench my thirst. he drank måny cups of tea, but cöuld not satisfy himsélf. he will soon bégín to quårrel with yòu ; but, if yòu ġive him a gentle answer, he will see his folly. yòu must gargle yòur mouth. his throat is much infllámed, and his töngue swóllen. they let down the anchör by means of the cáble. he stöod in the bow of the boat. her mouth is sore ; yòu must ġive her a little alum. yòu cannot swållòw so large a piece. take courage ; the wörst will soon be óver. he bound up his wóunds, póuring in oil and wine, and brought him to an inn.

65. The mark ˘ (called the *short mark*), püt óver åny letter, shóws that it is not in the same syllable as the letter befóre it. If the mark is on the first letter of a wörd, thát letter is not in the same syllable as the

next letter. The short mark, püt óver a vowel, shóws
also that the vowel is not silent, and that it has its
first sound.

bëïng	sëëth	wickĕd	nakĕd (nåkĕd)
easıĕr	rëăl	profīted	
easıĕst	leạrnĕd	vısïted	

66. When a wörd is separated by a hýphen, each
of its parts is sounded as a separate wörd; as,

shep-herd, fore-téll, fore-fäther.

67. When a w or y cömes betwéen twọ vowels, it
is to be sounded with the first, if thëre is no short
mark on the first vowel ; as,

drawer, drawing.

But if a short mark is püt on the first vowel, or a
hýphen after it, the w or y begíns the next syllable ; as,

ăwáy, re-wárd, be-yónd.

LESSON XXVII.

which of the two things is easıĕr for yòu tọ dọ?
whåt werẹ they sayıng tọ yòu? whåt sëëst thou
thëre ? he sëëth that they seethe flesh ın a large
cauldrön. yòu must leạrn dılıgently while yòu arẹ
yọung; and yòu wıll be the happıĕr for it as yòu gròw
up tọ manhöod. ıt wås a wıckĕd thıng tọ treat thát
poor óld man ın such a way. yòu wıll never be a
leạrnĕd man, ıf yòu arẹ an idle boy. all my toıl pro-
fīted me nöthıng. they requíted hıs grèat kindness
ın a very stränge and ungrâtefül way. she vısïted
me ın my sıckness ; and I am thankfül for her kindness. hıs bounty wås very grèat. hıs löve is rëăl.
rëälly I dọ not knòw. he töok my böok, and ran
ăwáy läughıng at me ; and, hıs legs bëïng lónger
than mıne, I cöuld not catch hım. whåt shall be my

re-wárd ? he walked ăwáy, be-yónd the sound of my
voice. I cöuld not make him hear whåt I meąnt tǫ
say. we cannot fore-téll fúturę événts. he ınhérıts
thát land from hıś fore-fäthers. I fore-sáw that yòu
wöuld be dıspléaśed wıth her conduct, bécáuśe she
dıd not condúct hersélf prúdently. the child ıś quıte
nakĕd. söme pressıng bųśıness called hım ăwáy from
home. yòu ǫught not tǫ snatch ăwáy' my böok.

68. Ăny combınâtıonś oͤf vowelś not ąlréądy men-
tıoned must be sounded ın twǫ syllableś, unléss ône
or more ıś marked aś bëïng sılent ; aś,

creáte	piety	rùın
crùel	póem	sciençe
	póet	violent

LESSON XXVIII.

arę yòu not gòıng tǫ sćhool ? he creátes grèat con-
fúśıon by hıś dıśórderly conduct. he tried hard tǫ
dècéıve us, but cöuld not succéed. he seemś tǫ be a
man of trùe piety. the child ıś quıte quiet now.
she haś a violent temper ; and thát ıś very trỳıng tǫ
her famıly. the poor child wåś crỳıng on accóunt of
the còld. he wåś an uṅkînd fäther, and a crùel
man. he wıll uśe threąts, but yòu must not mind hıś
violence. he struck hıś elbòw agâınst the chàır. she
wrote a bèautıfül pòem. I see no reaśön tǫ doubt
the rèálıty of the stòry. thát pòet haś grèat skıll.

69. The follówıng lıst contáıns wörds that arę
sounded alíke, though they arę wrıtten dıfferently.

àır	aught	bean	beer	berth
ёre	ǫught	been	bıer	bırth
hèır				
all	ball	beau	bell	boar
awl	bawl	bòw	belle	bore

bough	fain	knight	peal	seam
bow	fëign	night	peel	seem
bread	faint	knot	pole	sew
bred	fëint	not	pôll	so
brèwed	fair	knòw	pore	sòw
brood	fare	no	pòur	sight
çall	find	knòws	pray	site
çaul	fined	nose	prey	sloe
çause	foul	lead	rain	slòw
çaws	fowl	led	rëign	soar
çeil	hall	leak	rains	sore
seal	haul	leek	rëins	sole
chèws	hart	meat	right	sôul
choose	heart	meet	rite	söme
dear	hear	might	wright	sum
deer	here	mite	ring	sön
dew	heard	nay	wring	sun
due	herd	nëigh	road	thëir
die	him	nöne	rode	thëre
dye	hymn	nun	rôwed	thrèw
doe	hole	oar	roe	through
dough	whole	ore	rôw	thyme
döne	hour	pair	rose	time
dun	our	pare	rôws	tôld
ewe	in	peár	pause	tôlled
yew	inn	paws	scene	tön
you	knead	peace	seen	tun
eye	need	piece	sea	vain
I	knew		see	vëin
	new			

F

34

LESSON XXIX.

it is not right to write so badly, if you can do better.
he wrote a book about the rites of that strange
people. he is a wheel-wright. he rode on the high
road, while we rowed on the water. a brave knight
went forth on a moon-light night to seek the foe.
this tiny mite has but little might; we might find
thousands like it, in a small piece of decayed cheese.
if you will hold your peace, you shall have a piece of
cake. do you know how to knit? no; I do not
know. this knot is tied so tight, that I am not able
to untie it. my dear child, you must sit down, so;
while I sit and sew your new frock, and your father
goes out to sow some seeds in the garden. bow
your head a little, or else you will knock it against
that bough. you ought not to do aught of that kind.
he put the whole of it in a small hole. we shall fare
badly, unless we have fair weather. she knew that
the book was new. he will pore over his task, and
I will pour out the tea. there I saw their aunt. he
led me to a pipe of lead, that was made to lead away
the water. this is the heaviest rain we have had in
this king's reign; and, if it rains much longer, it will
spoil my new reins. what has he done with the dun
cow? he bore off the head of the boar. as soon as
I told him that the little girl was dead, he tolled the
bell. she is quite a belle. my dear boy, you shall
go with me, to see the deer in the park. they set
down the bier, and each of them drank a glass of
beer, before they bore the body to the grave. I will
pare these apples; and then I will give you a pear to
eat, while I fetch a pair of gloves. when he went to
ceil the room, he found a seal near the door. look
at the pretty lambs; but do not go near that ram,

lest he shöuld butt with his horns. the wagön brought a tun of wine and a tön of coals. he thrèw a stone through the window. he wås bred to a trade, but wås not àble to gain his bread by it. his sön and he walked in the sun, while we sat in the shade. do you see thát boat on the sea, and thát ewe, with her two lambs, near the yew tree? I feel a pain in my right èye. I asked the nun to sell me söme lace, but she tòld me they made nöne. löok at this ròw of fish, and exámine the roe of this fish. we six little girls sit in two ròws, and each has a rose. we aróse with the sun, and the boat-man, helped by his sön, ròws us on the water. though they cöuld find no law on the point, they fined him for his conduct. he wöuld fain have decéived me, and so bègán to fëign that he had never seen me befóre. we sought in vain for a vëin of metal. let each man take an oar, and we will soon row ăwáy with this boat-load of copper ore. it is not meet that you shöuld eat my meat. he bègán to haul up the packages that lay in the hall. he chèws his meat slòwly, while I take a long time to choose whåt I will eat. let us join him in singing thát hymn. if he shöuld call agâin, give him the caul of the sheep. he did nöthing but bawl, like a booby, when he lost his ball. she has no need to knead so much dough. we all must die önce. this man's trade is to dye wöol. withín an hour we shall reach our house. the tàste of the sloe is so tart, that I am slòw in eating a sloe-tart. she will knead the dough, while her husband kills the doe. pay me whåt is due to me. thère is a heavy dew. they stuck on a pole the numbers at the close of the pòll. the dog's nose is very göod; by it he knows whëre to find the game. listen to thát peal of bells. give me thát oraṅge-peel. I pray you do not becóme

* F 2

a prey tǫ anġer. we heạrd the lŏwing of the herd.
I cöuḷd not havẹ the hẹart tǫ kɪll thát nŏbḷe hart,
that the hunterś had been pursûing so long. she
döeś not seem tǫ ḳnòw how tǫ sėw a seam. sŏme
boyś wöuḷd soon dǫ thát sum. the sight of the
place wåś mòụrnfül tǫ me ; for the sɪte of the house
ɪn whɪch I wåś born wåś occúpied by standɪng corn.
all the flowerś of my prẹtty garden, whɪcḥ I had
nursed wɪth so much care, werẹ gonẹ. not a sòụl
wåś thëre ; I wåś the sole tenant of the place. I
wåś ɪn grèat paɪn, from the sole of my fŏot tǫ the
crown of my heạd. ɪt wåś a sɪlly feat, tǫ wạḷk wɪth
hɪś feet agåɪnst the ceɪlɪng. thɪs ɪś the fòụrth day
sɪnce he came fŏrih out of hɪś house. ɪt wåś the
ëigh'ih day after hɪś arrîval. I havẹ been löokɪng
for a bean, but can find ónly a pea. all that I cöuḷd
see wåś the shǫe-màker'ś awl. never sɪnce hɪś bɪrih·
dɪd he sleep ɪn so snug a berih. ɪn the place whëre
lie had brèwed hɪś ale, thëre wåś a brood of chɪckenś.
the cloih wåś so coarse, that of còụrse ɪt wåś much
cheaper than the öther. whåt ɪś the cauśe, that the
daw cawś so frèquently ? she made a fëɪnt that she
wåś gòɪng tǫ faɪnt. the weạther wåś so foul, that
not a fowl wöuḷd leave the yard. he came ɪn a
coach from the ɪnn. I trịed tǫ stop the leak ɪn the
boat, wɪth a leek from my basket. at a pauśe ɪn the
múśɪc the beạr raɪśed hɪś pawś. she bėgán tǫ wrɪng
her handś, aś soon aś she heạrd the bellś rɪng. such
a sad scene I had never seen bėfóre. the bɪrd cöuḷd
not soar. I had a sore leg. I had no tɪme tǫ fetch
ǎny thyme from the garden. Dɪd yòu hear the ass
bray ? nay ; I heạrd the horse nëɪgh. the weạther
wåś so fɪne, that he töok out hɪś sön and hėɪr, tǫ wạḷk
ɪn the sun and enjóy the wạrm àɪr ; but, ëre they had
been long out of the house, the wind chánged, and
the àɪr bėcáme quɪte còld.

70. The following list consists of words that are sounded differently, though they are spelled alike.

bow ⎰ bȯw ⎱	tear ⎰ tẹȧr ⎱	insult ⎰ˎ insúlt ⎱
cant ⎰ cän't ⎱	use ⎰ uṡe ⎱	object ⎰ objéct ⎱
close ⎰ cloṡe ⎱	excúse ⎰ excúṡe ⎱	present ⎰ présént ⎱
live ⎰ livẹ ⎱	absent ⎰ absént ⎱	produce ⎰ pródúce ⎱
liveṡ ⎰ livẹṡ ⎱	conduct ⎰ condúct ⎱	rebel ⎰ · rėbél ⎱
sow ⎰ sȯw ⎱·	deṡert ⎰ dėṡért ⎱	

LESSON XXX.

yȯu werẹ absent from school yesterday; yȯu must be cȧrẹfül not tọ absént yȯursélf äny more. dọ not prėténd tọ excúṡe yȯursélf; bėcáuṡe yȯu havẹ no good excúse tọ ġivẹ. she must leạrn tọ condúct hersélf in a better manner; or else her conduct will expóṡe her tọ grèat blame. he wås so crùel, aṡ tọ dėṡért his family, in the middle of the deṡert. he made a slight bow, and shot with his bȯw. the ȯld sow iṡ in the garden, whëre yȯu arẹ tọ sȯw the seedṡ. I saw a tear in her èye, when I wås gȯing tọ tẹȧr the letter. this böok iṡ of no use tọ me; for I dọ not knȯw how tọ uṡe it.   I cän't abíde such silly cant. we shall livẹ by selling live fish. he will not objéct tọ ġivẹ möney for so good an object. pródúce yȯur accóunts, and shȯw whåt produce yȯu havẹ sȯld. he livẹṡ by sȧving the liveṡ of öthers. dọ not insúlt him; he iṡ too passionate tọ bẹȧr äny insult. while my möther wås preṡent, they wished tọ présént me with a gȯld wåtch. the saucy little rebel did nöthing but

rebél agáinst my authórity. cloŝe the shutterŝ, and
oüt my chàır close tǫ the fıre-sıde.

71. Each oŕ the follówıng wördŝ haŝ twǫ or more
meanıngŝ, söme oŕ whıch havę no connectıon wıth
each öther.

beàr	- fleet	lay	net
bore	found	left	right
bound	graze	light	rush
crów	hóld	may	saw
dǫ	hıde	mean	sound
èven	kind	meanŝ	spoke
fàır	leave	mount	tell
fare	leaveŝ	neat	well

LESSON XXXI.

a whıte beàr can beàr grèat cóld. he bore grèat
fatígue, when he had tǫ bore a deep well. the
lıttle anımal wâŝ bound ; and so ıt cöuļd not bound
ın ıts üŝùal way. ıt wıll not dǫ for hım tǫ dǫ so an
öther tıme. ıt ıŝ hard tǫ waļk so fast, èven on èven
ground. we saw sundry fàır damŝelŝ at the fàır.
we had but poor fare tǫ eat ; aŝ we werę oblíged tǫ
keep söme mönęy, tǫ pay our fare tǫ the boat-man.
the horse wâŝ fleet ; but cöuļd not óvertáke the man,
befóre he wâŝ safe on board ône oŕ the vesselŝ ın the
fleet. he found a suffícıent quàntıty oŕ metal, tǫ
found a staţue oŕ the persön, whǫ had döne so much
göod, and whǫ had wıshed tǫ found a hospıtal ın hıŝ
nàtıve town. the horse had begún tǫ graze, when a
shot wâŝ fıred, whıch happenęd tǫ graze hıŝ right
ear. we cöuļd not püt more wheat ıntǫ the hóld oŕ
the shıp, for ıt wöuļd hóld no more. he had stólen
a bullock's hıde ; whıch he attémpted tǫ hıde ın the
roof oŕ hıŝ cottage. ıt wâŝ not kind tǫ act ın thát
kind oŕ way. he gave her leave tǫ go, but she

wöuld not leave her child. she leaves her children
in the garden; and they amúse themsélves in gather-
ing leaves. I will lay down my blanket here, in the
place whëre I lay last night. he lost his right hand;
but his left hand is still left quite unhúrt. the load
is light; and we hope to reach the end of our journey,
befóre we lose the light of the moon. I do not
think he cöuld mean to act in so mean a way. we
cannot see by whåt means he means to perfórm his
task. we shall mount our horses, and ride to the
top of the mount. she is a neat dairy-wöman, and
her husband has a göod måny neat cattle. it is not
right to use your left hand instéad of your right. do
not rush hástily into the water; but go slówly in, and
gather for me the tallest rush you can find. we saw
them hard at wörk with a long saw. she struck the
básin, to try if it were sound, and knew it wås so, by
the sound it gave. thëre are måny vessels in the
sound, and söme of them will soon püt to sea.
I spoke to the wheel-wright, to make me a new
spoke or two. we cannot till the land till the
frost is gone. I am not well enóugh to fetch water
from the well. the cock will crów, and the crów
will croak. in the mönth of May we may have
warm weather. though they caught måny fish in
each net, yet the net value to thëir emplóyers wås
not gréat.

whåt ails this field of wheat? it has been beaten
down by the hail. you must not go into the air
withóut söme cövering on your hair. he drinks too
much ale; but he löoks quite hale and hearty. all
the family are at the hall. alter this bit, while I püt
the halter on the mule. I am not fond of ham. he

your eye on high, and hand me down thát plum.
we will sit in this arbour, and löok at the ships in the
harbour.   my arm has táken no harm.   he found an
arrow, when he went to harrów thát field.   he must
use söme art in cöming near thát hart.   when you
have cut down the ash you shall have söme hash for
dinner.   when you sit at table you must not keep
on your hat.   with his left ear he cannot hear much.
eat söme of this meat, while I heat the tart.   I must
püt an edge to my bill, and then lower this hedge.
he found an eel under his right heel.   this piece of
elm will make a göod helm.   a wöoden ewer will
suit a hewer of wöod.   I am so ill that I cannot
mount the hill.   his ire is grèat, becáuse you will not
hire him.   it is his fault.   it will hit you.   my oar
is cövered by hoar frost.   thát öld nail will not höld.
on the ösier bed the hösier laid the stockings.   the
otter döes not wish the water hotter.